This book belongs to

· · · · · · · · · · · · · · · · · ·

For Gabriella

DK

A DORLING KINDERSLEY BOOK

First American Edition, 1993   10 9 8 7 6 5 4 3 2 1

Published in the United States by
Dorling Kindersley, Inc., 232 Madison Avenue, New York, New York 10016

Library of Congress Cataloging-Publication Data
Winter, Susan.
    Me too / by Susan Winter. — 1st American ed.
        p. cm.
    Summary: A young girl likes trying to do all the things
her big brother can do.
    ISBN 1-56458-198-5
    [1. Brothers and sisters—Fiction. 2. Growth—Fiction.]
I. Title.
PZ7.W7625Me 1993
[E]—dc20
                                                    92-53483
                                                       CIP
                                                       AC

Color reproduction by Dot Gradations
Printed in Belgium by Proost

ME TOO

Susan Winter

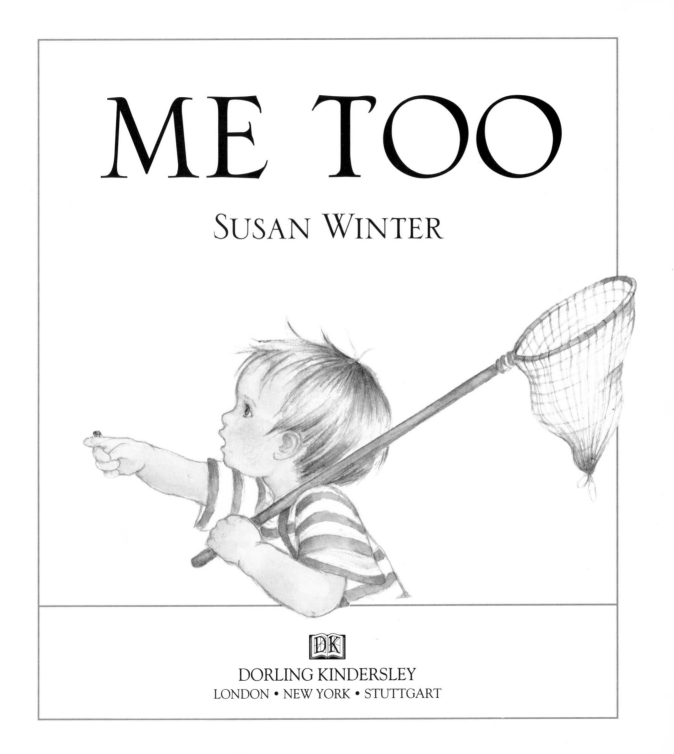

DK

DORLING KINDERSLEY

LONDON • NEW YORK • STUTTGART

My brother is really smart. . .

He likes reading.

Me too.

He likes building blocks.

Me too.

He likes writing.

Me too.

He likes dressing up.

Me too.

He likes jumping rope.

Me too.

He likes running.

Me too.

He likes bugs.

Me too.

He likes watching scary movies.

Me too.

He likes doing magic tricks.

Me too.

He needs me.